Welcome to Planet Reader!

Invite your child on a journey to a wonderful, imaginative place—the limitless universe of reading! And there's no better traveling companion than you, the parent. Every time you and your child read together you send out an important message: Reading can be rewarding and *fun*. This understanding is essential to helping your child build the skills and confidence he or she needs as an emerging reader.

Here are some tips for sharing Planet Reader stories with your child:

Be open! Some children like to listen to or read the whole story and then ask questions. Some children will stop on every page with a question or a comment. Either way is fine; the most important thing is that your child feels reading is a pleasurable experience.

Be understanding! Sometimes your child might need a direct answer. If he or she points to a word and asks you to tell what it is, do so. Other times, your child may want to sound out a word or stop to figure out a sentence independently. Allow for both approaches.

Enjoy! The story and characters in this book were created especially for your child's age group. Talk about the story. Take turns reading favorite parts. Look at how the illustrations support the story and enhance the reading experience.

And most of all, enjoy your child's journey into literacy. It's one of the most important trips the two of you will ever take!

For Hope Slaughter Bryant, Judy Cunningham,
Mary Hanson, Judith Herold, Ellen Kelley,
Marni McGee, and Lisa Merkl:
with love and thanks for
making Fridays Tyranno-rrific!
—L.W.

For my nephew, Jamie.
—J.D.

Text copyright © 1998 by Lee Wardlaw Jaffurs.
Illustrations copyright © 1998 by Julie Durrell.

Published by Troll Communications L.L.C.

Planet Reader is a trademark of Troll Communications L.L.C.

Printed in the United States of America.   ISBN 0-8167-4434-3

10   9   8   7   6   5   4   3

This edition reprinted by permission of Troll Communications L.L.C.

Dinosaur Pizza

by Lee Wardlaw

illustrated by Julie Durrell

It's the first day of school.

It's the *worst* day of school.

My best friend, Anna, moved away.

I have to wait for the bus alone.

Then I lose my lucky stegosaurus.

The one Anna gave me.

In class, everyone sits next to a best
friend. I'm stuck sitting next to the
hamster cage.

At lunch, I have no one to share
my peanut butter-and-banana
sandwiches. Anna used to call them
PBBs.

"Howdy, partner," says a girl. "I'm Bobbi Jo, president of the Lunch Bunch Club. Would you like to join?"

"What are the rules?" I ask.

"There are four," says Bobbi Jo. "One, you have to eat lunch with us every day. Two, you have to share your lunch. Three, you must bring good things to eat."

"What's Number Four?" I ask.

"You have to obey rules One, Two, and Three. Or else we kick you out."

"Count me in!" I grab my lunch bag and hurry after Bobbi Jo.

"I want you to meet the Lunch
Bunch," she says. "This is Duke."

"Yo," says Duke.

"And this is Winston."

"It's Monday," Winston warns.

"I eat only green food on Monday."

"Chow time!" Bobbi Jo shouts.

"Yay!" says Duke.

Bobbi Jo tucks a napkin under her chin. She opens a picnic basket. It's filled with buffalo chili, corn bread, and dandelion salad.

Winston opens a bag that reads *Monday.* He's packed pea soup, lime Jell-O, and pickles. For dessert he has a bag of M&Ms. Green ones.

"Kiwi juice?" Winston offers.

"Uh, no thanks," I answer.

Duke whisks out a toolbox with a lock. He sneaks a peek at me. Then he fiddles with the dial. He lifts the lid.

The smell of Chinese food tickles my nose.

"Are those real chopsticks?" I ask.

"Yup," says Duke.

Bobbi Jo points at my lunch bag.

"What do *you* have to share?"

"An apple, a cupcake, and two

PBBs," I say.

"Yawn," says Duke.

"Don't you have anything green?"

Winston asks.

I shake my head.

Winston sighs.

11

"She'll do better tomorrow," says
Bobbi Jo. *"Won't you?"*
"Does anyone want to hear a
dinosaur joke?" I ask.
The Lunch Bunchers don't answer.
They are too busy swapping lunches
to notice me.

That night, Mom brings home pizza for dinner. I tell her I'm not hungry.

"I miss Anna," I say.

"I know," says Mom. "You'll make new friends soon. I promise."

"Can I take something different for lunch tomorrow?" I ask.

"I thought you liked PBBs."

"I did. I do. But sometimes a person wants a change."

"All right," says Mom.

"Oh, and I'll need something green."

"*Green?*" Mom asks.

"Green," I say.

The next day, Bobbi Jo brings armadillo stew, yam fritters, and shoofly pie.

Winston eats scrambled eggs with mustard, corn-on-the-cob, and lemon bars.

"Pineapple salsa?" he offers.

"Uh, no thanks," I say.

Duke unlocks his toolbox.

I smell something spicy.

"Is that a real sombrero?" I ask.

"Yup," says Duke.

Bobbi Jo points at my lunch bag.

"What do *you* have to share?"

"An apple, three cookies, and a
chicken sandwich."

"Yawn," says Duke.

"Don't you have anything yellow?"
Winston asks.

"No," I say. "But look! I brought you
a green apple."

Winston sighs. "Today is Tuesday.
I eat only yellow food on Tuesday."

"Oh," I say. "What color is
Wednesday?"

Winston gives me a don't-you-know-
anything? look.

"Red," he says.

"When is blue day?" I ask.

"Yuck," says Duke.

Winston wrinkles his nose. "Who would eat *blue* food?"

"Someone's forgotten rule Number Four," warns Bobbi Jo.

I gulp. "I'll do better tomorrow. Honest."

That night, I don't sleep well. I dream
the Lunch Bunchers are eating with
Anna. *And* my lucky stegosaurus.
I'm eating lunch with the hamster.

The next morning, I tell Mom I want
to make my own lunch.

"Well . . ." she says. "I don't know."

I cross my heart. "I promise, no
candy-bar sandwiches. No potato-chip
soup. No chocolate-chip salad. Deal?"

"Deal," says Mom.

I open the refrigerator. There are lots of leftovers inside. I pull out packets and tubs. Baggies and jars. I pile them all on the table. Then I set to work.

For lunch, Bobbi Jo brings opossum
jerky, grits with red-eye gravy, and
creamed okra.

Winston eats cherry soup and a
ketchup sandwich.

"Beet smoothie?" he offers.

"Uh, no thanks," I say.

Duke unlocks his toolbox. Then
he tucks a flower behind his ear.
"Is that a real Hawaiian lei?" I ask.
"Yup," says Duke.

Bobbi Jo frowns at my lunch bag.
"What do *you* have to share? And it
better be *good*."

I shrug. "Oh, just some leftover
Dinosaur Pizza."

"Dinosaur Pizza?!"

The Lunch Bunchers crowd
around me.

Each one grabs a slice.

They chomp and chew and smack
their lips.

"Yum!" says Duke.

"It's red!" cries Winston.

"I've never eaten dinosaur before,"
Bobbi Jo says. "It tastes like chicken."

I hide a smile.

Bobbi Jo licks her fingers. "I can't
wait till tomorrow!"

"Tomorrow?" I squeak.

"Tomorrow," says Bobbi Jo. "Top this, and the Lunch Bunchers will make you a lifetime member. If not . . ."

She doesn't finish her sentence.

I gulp.

"Don't forget," Winston says.

"Thursday is brown day."

"Yup," says Duke. He bites into another slice of Dinosaur Pizza.

After school, I hurry to the library.
I think about the Lunch Bunch. And
dinosaurs. And food that is brown.
Then I read cookbook after cookbook.
That night, Mom helps me make
a super-duper lunch.

"What's that?" Bobbi Jo asks the
next day at lunch.

"It's a volcano cake," I answer.

"Would you like a piece?"

I take out a glass of magic stuff.

I pour it into the mouth of the
volcano.

The volcano sputters and burbles.

Bubbles and steams.

"Yikes!" yells Duke.

"It's erupting!" Winston cries.

"Thar she blows!" screams Bobbi Jo.

She dives under the table.

At last the smoke clears.

I cut a slice of volcano for everyone.

"Yay!" says Duke.

"Delicious lava," says Winston.

Bobbi Jo crawls out from under the table. "Hee-haw! What are you bringing for lunch tomorrow?"

"I have other plans," I say.

"Don't forget rule Number Four," warns Bobbi Jo.

"I haven't," I answer. "But sometimes a person wants a change."

Tomorrow, I think I'll look for my lucky stegosaurus. Write a letter to Anna. Or feed the hamster. Or I might want to be alone with a tasty PBB . . .

. . . and for dessert, a slice of Dinosaur Pizza.

Dinosaur Pizza

You will need:

1 adult to help you
1 small jar pizza sauce
1 small package ready-made pizza shells
   (individual size, two shells in each
   package)
1 cup (.24 l) grated mozzarella cheese
1 small can whole black olives
   (drained)
1 small jar whole green olives (drained)
1 small package pepperoni slices
1 green bell pepper, cut into small
   triangles (to look like fangs)
1 cookie sheet or baking stone
1 pizza cutter or sharp knife

1. Preheat the oven to 450 degrees F (230°C).

2. Spoon a thin layer of pizza sauce onto each pizza shell. Sprinkle ½ cup (.12 l) mozzarella cheese on top of the sauce on each shell.

3. To make a dinosaur face, use two black olives for eyes and two green olives for nostrils. Pepperoni slices can be used to make rosy cheeks. Arrange the pepper "fangs" to look like the dinosaur's mouth is open.

4. Place the pizzas on the cookie sheet or baking stone. Bake for eight to ten minutes, or until the cheese bubbles. Remove from the oven and cool for a couple of minutes before slicing.

Serves two.

To create different dinosaur faces, experiment with zucchini, mushroom, or onion slices, chunks of pineapple, cooked chicken or meatballs, canned corn kernels . . . or whatever tasty leftovers you find in your refrigerator!